ST. AGNES SCHOOL
Springfield, Illinois

D1308792

# BUTTONYMS
# FOR
# SAFETY

## A
## FABLES FROM THE LETTER PEOPLE
## BOOK

WRITTEN BY:
ELAYNE REISS-WEIMANN
RITA FRIEDMAN

ILLUSTRATED BY:
ELIZABETH CALLEN

**NEW DIMENSIONS IN EDUCATION, INC.**
**50 EXECUTIVE BLVD.**
**ELMSFORD, NY 10523**

Copyright © 1989 New Dimensions in Education, Inc.

All rights reserved.

No part of this publication may be reproduced, stored in a retrieval system, or transmitted, in any form or by any means, electronic, mechanical, photocopying, recording, or otherwise, without the prior written permission of the publishers.

Printed in U.S.A.

ISBN 0-89796-001-7

1  2  3  4  5  6  7  8  9  0     SPC     SPC     89098     13502

Every Saturday, Mr. B wheels his beautiful buttons
to Bingo's house for a visit.
One Saturday, the beautiful buttons do not want
to be wheeled in their big basket.
"Mr. B, we want to walk beside you," they say.
"All right," says Mr. B, "let's walk together."

1

The beautiful buttons walk along beside Mr. B.

Then Benjamin Button sits down.

"I'm too tired to walk anymore," he says.

"Please carry me, Mr. B."

Mr. B bends down to pick up Benjamin Button.

The other beautiful buttons do not wait for Mr. B.

They run away to Bingo's house.

By the time Mr. B looks up, they are gone.

Mr. B runs after the beautiful buttons.

But he cannot run fast carrying Benjamin Button.

The beautiful buttons get to Bingo's house first.

"Where is Mr. B?" asks Bingo Bunny.

"We didn't wait for him," answer the buttons.

Suddenly, Bingo hears Mr. B shouting,

"Bingo, Bingo, did you see the beautiful buttons?"

"Mr. B, here we are!" call the beautiful buttons.

"Running away was a very bad thing to do,"
scolds Mr. B.

"We didn't think we were being bad.
Why can't we walk by ourselves?" they ask.

"You must never run away from me," says Mr. B.

"It is not safe.

You could be hurt.

I don't want that to happen to you.

Let's talk about rules for walking safely."

"Rules, rules, rules!

There are always rules," say the beautiful buttons.

"We can use another name for rules," says Mr. B.

"Instead of following rules,

buttons will follow buttonyms."

"Buttonyms!
We like that," smile the beautiful buttons.
"Now listen carefully to the buttonym
for walking safely," says Mr. B.
        "Buttonym: Stay near me and never run away."
"We'll stay near you, and we'll never run away,"
say the beautiful buttons.
"Mr. B, let's take another walk.
We'll show you we can walk safely."
"That's a good idea," smiles Mr. B.

9

"Bingo," says Mr. B, "we will be back
in a little while."
Mr. B and the beautiful buttons walk up one street
and down another.
They keep saying the buttonym for walking safely:
"Stay near Mr. B and never run away.
Stay near Mr. B and never run away."
Mr. B turns and walks toward a busy street.
The buttons follow him.

Mr. B stops at a traffic light.

The buttons stop.

"Why do we have to stop?" asks Benjamin Button.

"I must look at the traffic light," answers Mr. B.

"The traffic light is a signal.

It tells us when it is safe to cross.

But before we cross, I had better teach you

the buttonyms for crossing the street safely,"

says Mr B.

13

"Listen carefully to these buttonyms," says Mr. B.
"Buttonym: Always cross the street
with a grown-up.
Buttonym: Go when the traffic light is green.
Stop when the traffic light is red.
I know a song about traffic lights," says Mr. B.
Then Mr. B sings, "Green lights are 'go' lights.
They are 'cross' lights.
They are 'yes' lights.
Red lights are 'stop' lights.
They are 'wait' lights.
They are 'no' lights."

The beautiful buttons sing Mr. B's song.
Then Benjamin says, "I made up my own song:
    The traffic light is red or green.
    And I know what those colors mean.
    Green says, 'Benjamin, GO! GO! GO!'
    Red says, 'Benjamin, NO! NO! NO!' "
"Benjamin, that's a wonderful song," smiles Mr. B.
"But remember, always cross with a grown-up."
Everyone walks back to Bingo's house singing
Benjamin's song.

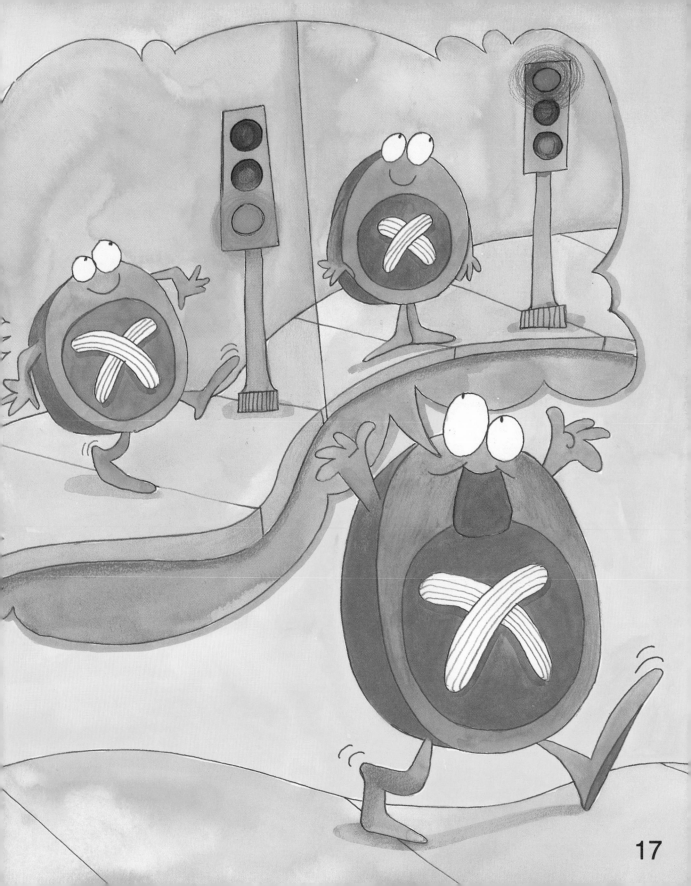

17

The buttons tell Bingo about their walk.
Then Mr. B says, "I'll be back at four o'clock
to take the beautiful buttons home."
"Bingo," say the buttons, "we want to make a book
of the buttonyms we learned and give it to Mr. B."
Bingo gives them crayons and paper.
They draw pictures about the buttonyms.
Bingo helps them make a buttonym book.
Just before four o'clock the beautiful buttons
go outside to wait for Mr. B.
Benjamin carries the buttonym book.

Suddenly, a big, shiny car drives up and stops beside
the beautiful buttons.
A smiling lady says, "Get into my car,
and I will take you home."
"We don't know you," says Barbie Button.
"We had better wait for Mr. B."
"Mr. B asked me to bring you to him, and I have candy
and toys for you, too," smiles the lady.
"May I look at your book?" she asks Benjamin,
as she opens the car door.

Benjamin hands the book to the stranger.

He starts to get into the stranger's car.

Barbie grabs Benjamin's arm.

"Benjamin! Stay right here with me," she shouts.

"Run and get Bingo," she yells to the other buttons.

The lady sees the buttons running into the house.

She slams the car door and speeds away.

Just then Mr. B arrives.

Mr. B sees the buttons running.

He sees Benjamin crying.

"What's wrong?" asks Mr. B, picking up Benjamin.

"The buttonym book we made for you is gone," cries Benjamin.

Barbie Button tells Mr. B about the car, the lady, the toys, the candy, and the buttonym book.

"We'll make another buttonym book," says Mr. B.

"We'll put in buttonyms about strangers.

Now let's go into Bingo's house."

The buttons listen as Mr. B talks to them.
"Listen carefully to these buttonyms
about strangers," he says.
        "Buttonym: Never go anywhere with a stranger.
    Buttonym: Never get into a stranger's car.
    Buttonym: Never take candy or toys
                from a stranger.
    Buttonym: Try to find someone you know to help
                you if a stranger bothers you.
Barbie was smart to send for Bingo."

"There are a lot of buttonyms about strangers,"
says Benjamin.
"And you must remember all of them," says Mr. B.
"We will try," say the beautiful buttons.
But Benjamin doesn't say anything.
Benjamin isn't there.
"Benjamin, where are you?" calls Mr. B.
"I'm making a big new buttonym book," says Benjamin.
"We want to help you," say the other buttons.
"There are a lot of buttonyms to draw."

29

"Our buttonym book will keep getting bigger
and bigger," says Mr. B.
"There will always be more buttonyms for safety.
And I will always be here to teach them to you
and to help you learn them."
Then Mr. B gives each of the beautiful buttons
a big button hug.

## DATE DUE

| | | | |
|---|---|---|---|
| | | | |
| | | | |
| | | | |
| | | | |
| | | | |
| | | | |
| | | | |
| | | | |
| | | | |
| | | | |
| | | | |
| | | | |
| | | | |
| | | | |
| | | | |
| | | | |
| | | | |

DEMCO 38-297